A CHICK 'n' PUG Christmas

For Fejster, 'cause it just wouldn't be Christmas without him

First published in the United States of America in September 2014
by Bloomsbury Children's Books
www.bloomsbury.com

Bloomsbury is a registered trademark of Bloomsbury Publishing Plc

For information about permission to reproduce selections from this book, write to
Permissions, Bloomsbury Children's Books, 1385 Broadway, New York, New York 10018
Bloomsbury books may be purchased for business or promotional use. For information on bulk purchases
please contact Macmillan Corporate and Premium Sales Department at specialmarkets@macmillan.com

Library of Congress Cataloging-in-Publication Data
Sattler, Jennifer Gordon, author, illustrator.
A Chick 'n' Pug Christmas / by Jennifer Sattler.
pages   cm
Summary: Sidekick Chick's new mission for his best friend—and hero—Pug, who would rather sleep, involves dressing as Santa and spreading joy to everyone at Christmas.
ISBN 978-1-59990-602-7 (hardcover) • ISBN 978-1-61963-262-2 (e-book) • ISBN 978-1-61963-463-3 (e-PDF)
[1. Christmas—Fiction. 2. Roosters—Fiction. 3. Pug—Fiction. 4. Dogs—Fiction. 5. Friendship—Fiction. 6. Humorous stories.] I. Title. II. Title: Chick and Pug Christmas.
PZ7.S24935Chk 2014   [E]—dc23   2014005021

Art created with acrylics and colored pencil
Typeset in Cafeteria and Draftsman Casual
Book design by Nicole Gastonguay

Printed in China by Leo Paper Products, Heshan, Guangdong
2 4 6 8 10 9 7 5 3 1

All papers used by Bloomsbury Publishing, Inc., are natural, recyclable products made from wood grown in well-managed forests.
The manufacturing processes conform to the environmental regulations of the country of origin.

A CHICK 'n' PUG
Christmas

Jennifer Sattler

BLOOMSBURY

NEW YORK   LONDON   NEW DELHI   SYDNEY

It was December and Chick was chilly.

But his hero and best friend,
Pug, was toasty warm.

"Boy, what a super-fuzzy hat, Pug,"
said Chick as he snuggled up to him.
"This is quite an outfit."

"It's kind of itchy . . . ," mumbled Pug,

"but I guess I have the tummy for it."

"I'm supposed to look like Santa Claus," said Pug.

"He brings presents and spreads joy to everyone at Christmas. And . . . he has a large tummy."

"Wow," whispered Chick. "Does he have big muscles? How does he deliver everything in one night?"

"He flies through the sky," said Pug with a yawn.

"So he's a **superhero!**
Does he have a **sidekick?**"

"Well," said Pug, "he does have elves."

"Ooh! Ooh! I want to be an elf! Can I? Can I?"

"Do the elves spread joy too? Do they jump out and yell, 'SURPRISE! HERE'S SOME JOY!'?"

"Nope," said Pug. "There's definitely NO yelling."

"Look!" shouted Chick. "It's the Dude!
Let's spread some joy on him!"

Pug sighed. "Guess nap
time's over."

Chick searched high and low for the
perfect gift. "Here ya go, Dude! Fetch!"

"Merry Christmas, Dude! Let's go spread some more joy!"

Chick stopped in his tracks.

Aww! My wittle weindeer is just adorable!

Up ahead was their old nemesis, Mr. Snuggles.

"Spreading joy can be a dangerous job. Good thing we're fearless superheroes."

"Pug, are you thinking
what I'm thinking?"
"I doubt it," mumbled Pug.

"Now everyone will know where you are! Merry Christmas, Mr. Snuggles!" shouted Chick.

Soon they came across an ordinary citizen who
looked like he was in need of some holiday cheer.
"We'd be *nuts* not to help. Get it, Pug?"

Chick got right to work.
"Fear not, my friend! Help is
on the way!"

"No need to thank us. Just doin' our job.
Merry Christmas!"
"Nap time," said Pug.

While Pug napped, Chick realized something. He hadn't gotten a present for his best friend. He thought . . .

. . . and he thought.

And soon he had an idea.

"Pug! Wake up! I have a surprise for you!"

"Merry Christmas, Pug!" shouted Chick. "Every superhero needs a mask!"

"Thanks, little buddy. I'll use it all the time."

"What would Santa and his elves do now, Pug?" asked Chick.

"Well, I guess they'd fly back to the North Pole in Santa's sleigh."

"Hmm," thought Chick.

"But we don't have a . . ."

"Pug, look!"

"Merry Christmas, everyone!"

"Santa!"